# Dear Parent:

Congratulations! Your child is taking the first steps on an exciting journey. The destination? Independent reading!

**STEP INTO READING®** will help your child get there. The program offers books at five levels that accompany children from their first attempts at reading to reading success. Each step includes fun stories, fiction and nonfiction, and colorful art. There are also Step into Reading Sticker Books, Step into Reading Math Readers, Step into Reading Write-In Readers, Step into Reading Phonics Readers, and Step into Reading Phonics First Steps! Boxed Sets—a complete literacy program with something to interest every child.

## Learning to Read, Step by Step!

**Ready to Read   Preschool–Kindergarten**
• big type and easy words • rhyme and rhythm • picture clues
For children who know the alphabet and are eager to begin reading.

**Reading with Help   Preschool–Grade 1**
• basic vocabulary • short sentences • simple stories
For children who recognize familiar words and sound out new words with help.

**Reading on Your Own   Grades 1–3**
• engaging characters • easy-to-follow plots • popular topics
For children who are ready to read on their own.

**Reading Paragraphs   Grades 2–3**
• challenging vocabulary • short paragraphs • exciting stories
For newly independent readers who read simple sentences with confidence.

**Ready for Chapters   Grades 2–4**
• chapters • longer paragraphs • full-color art
For children who want to take the plunge into chapter books but still like colorful pictures.

**STEP INTO READING®** is designed to give every child a successful reading experience. The grade levels are only guides. Children can progress through the steps at their own speed, developing confidence in their reading, no matter what their grade.

Remember, a lifetime love of reading starts with a single step!

*To my nephew,*
*William*

www.stepintoreading.com

Educators and librarians, for a variety of teaching tools, visit us at
www.randomhouse.com/teachers

Library of Congress Cataloging-in-Publication Data
Shealy, Dennis R.
The Incredible Dash / by Dennis "Rocket" Shealy; designed by Disney's Global Design Group.
p. cm. — (Step into reading. A step 3 book)
Summary: The Incredibles, a family which appears normal but whose members have super
powers, confront the evil Syndrome.
ISBN 0-7364-2265-X (trade) — ISBN 0-7364-8033-1 (lib. bdg.)
[1. Heroes—Fiction. 2. Identity—Fiction.] I. Disney Global Artists. II. Title. III. Series:
Step into reading. Step 3 book.
PZ7.S53767In 2004
[E]—dc22
2004002083

Printed in the United States of America  30  29  28  27

STEP INTO READING, RANDOM HOUSE, and the Random House colophon are registered trademarks of
Random House, Inc.

Disney PRESENTS A PIXAR FILM

# THE INCREDIBLES

# THE INCREDIBLE DASH

Adapted by Dennis "Rocket" Shealy

Illustrated by the Disney Storybook Artists

Designed by Disney Publishing's Global Design Group

Inspired by the art and character designs created by
Pixar Animation Studios

Random House 🏠 New York

Hi! My name is Dash.

I am a Super.

I have Super powers.

I can run faster

than anyone I know.

I can show off my Super speed
when I'm in my Super suit.
But when I run on the track team,
I pretend to be normal.
I don't want to blow my cover.
I always win second place.

When we are normal,

Dad goes to work.

Mom takes care of Jack-Jack.

My sister, Vi,

and I go to school.

Other times,

we put on our Super suits

and fight the bad guys!

We always win,

because we're really . . .

# THE INCREDIBLES!

Before I was born, Supers ruled!
They kept the world
safe from bad guys.
My dad was Mr. Incredible.
He was the best Super
and always wanted to work alone.

My mom, Elastigirl,

was famous, too.

She could slug a criminal

from down the block.

Then the Supers got into trouble.

People stopped wanting

to be saved.

They started thinking that

the Supers caused problems.

They told the Supers

to quit being heroes.

The Supers went into hiding.

They pretended to be normal.

Mr. Incredible became Bob Parr.

Elastigirl became Helen Parr.

Then they had us kids.

Vi and I were Supers,

but Jack-Jack was normal.

Vi could turn invisible.

She also made force fields.

Vi and I sometimes used

our Super powers when we argued.

Mom had a problem with that.

Mom had bigger problems with Dad.

He still wanted to be a Super.

One time his boss would not

let him save someone.

Dad gave him a tiny push.

But it was a Super push.

Dad lost his job.

Then Dad got a message

to go on a top-secret mission.

Dad wanted to go.

He kept it a secret.

If Dad got caught

being a Super,

our family would have

to move again.

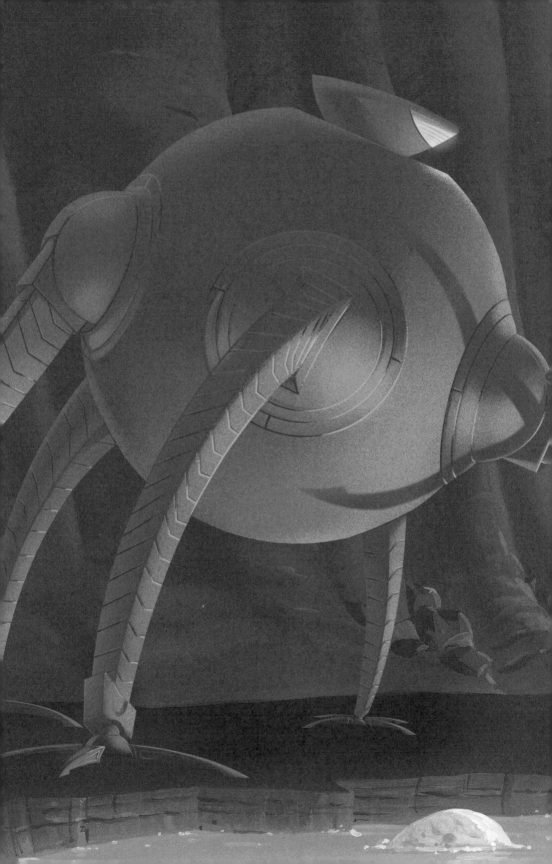

Dad's mission was

to defeat a big robot.

It was called the Omnidroid.

The Omnidroid was a smart robot.

It was really hard to beat.

But Dad was still the best Super.

He tricked the robot and won!

Then Dad got

more secret hero work.

This time, there was

a more powerful Omnidroid.

It defeated Dad!

That's when Dad found out
that his boss was a bad guy!
His name was Syndrome.
He created the Omnidroids.

Syndrome wanted to be a Super.

He had a big plan.

He would send the Omnidroid

to attack the city.

Then he would defeat

the Omnidroid himself

and look like a Super.

Dad found Syndrome's computer.

He learned that Syndrome

had destroyed most of the Supers.

Then Syndrome caught him!

Mom figured out that

Dad had not been going to work.

She was really mad.

Mom packed her Super suit.

She had to go find Dad.

Vi and I got Super suits, too.

But we had to stay home.

Vi and I snuck onto Mom's jet.

Mom was not happy about that.

But before she got too angry,

Syndrome attacked us.

We landed safely in the ocean.

Then Mom became a boat.

I got to be the motor!

I used my Super speed.

When we reached the shore,

Mom left Violet and me in a cave.

For the first time ever,

she told us to use our powers

if the bad guys found us.

Cool!

Mom went to save Dad.
My mom's stretching powers
are awesome.

Meanwhile, I explored the cave.

I saw a huge ball of fire.

Violet and I ran for our lives!

We made it out of the cave.

Then Syndrome's guards

raced after us.

Violet turned invisible.

I ran Super fast!

Mom found Dad.
They figured out
we were in trouble.
They raced to the rescue.

I could see why they had been

the best Supers ever!

They were surprised at how Super

Violet and I were, too.

We were one Super family!

Then Syndrome trapped us.
He used one of his inventions,
since he's not a real Super.

Now Syndrome was ready
to go through with his plan.
He headed into the city
to pretend to defeat
his own robot.

After Syndrome took off,

Vi slipped into her force field

and escaped.

She set us free, too.

Now we had to stop Syndrome!

I saw one of
Syndrome's rockets.
It was the only thing
that could get
us to the city in time.

Meanwhile, the Omnidroid

was wrecking the city.

Syndrome pretended

to fight the giant robot with

his remote control.

People cheered for him.

His plan was working!

The Omnidroid figured out that
Syndrome was controlling it.
It knocked out Syndrome
and the remote control.

Mom had been holding a
camper to the rocket.
When she let go,
we headed right toward
Syndrome and the Omnidroid.

We soared toward the city
in the camper.
We got there just in time!

Dad wanted to fight alone,

just the way he used to.

But Mom said we were a family.

We'd have to fight together.

And that's just what we did!

The crowd cheered for us,
but our work wasn't done yet.

Syndrome kidnapped Jack-Jack.

But Jack-Jack turned

into a fireball,

then into a Super-strong

little monster.

He was a Super, too.

We defeated Syndrome!

Awesome!

We have the best family!

We still pretend to be normal.

But when a villain bullies the world,

my family—THE INCREDIBLES—

is there to save the day!